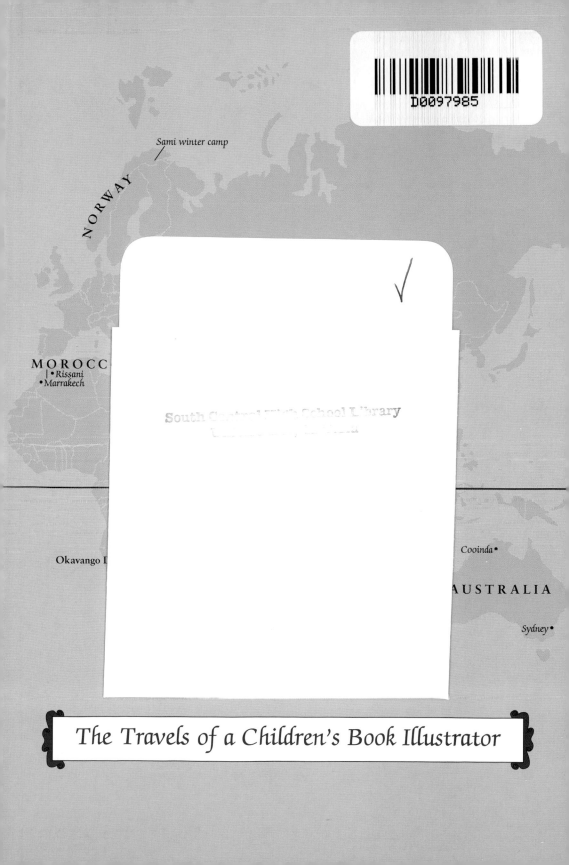

Sami winter camp

NORWAY

MOROCC
| •Rissani
•Marrakech

Okavango I

Cooinda •

AUSTRALIA

Sydney •

The Travels of a Children's Book Illustrator

TOUCH AND GO

Touch and Go

Travels of a Children's Book Illustrator

TED LEWIN

LOTHROP, LEE & SHEPARD BOOKS • NEW YORK

To Sheila Youthed,
and in memory of her husband, Syd

Published by Lothrop, Lee & Shepard Books
a division of William Morrow and Company, Inc.
1350 Avenue of the Americas, New York, NY 10019
www.williammorrow.com

Printed in the United States of America.
10 9 8 7 6 5 4 3 2 1

Library of Congress Cataloging-in-Publication Data
Lewin, Ted.
Touch and go: travels of a children's book illustrator/Ted Lewin.
p. cm.
Summary: The author-illustrator describes some of the most memorable people and places he has encountered in his travels.
ISBN 0-688-14109-9 (RTE)
1. Lewin, Ted-Journeys-Juvenile literature. 2. Illustrators-United States-Biography-Juvenile literature. [1. Lewin, Ted. 2. Illustrators. 3. Voyages and travels.] I. Title.
NC975.5.L38A2 1999 741.6'42'092 [b]-DC21 98-40548 CIP AC
ISBN 0-688-14109-9 (RTE)

The painting of "Norway: *Lavu* at Sami winter camp" is reprinted with the permission of Simon & Schuster Books for Young Readers, an imprint of Simon & Schuster Children's Publishing Division, from *The Reindeer People*, written and illustrated by Ted Lewin.

PICTURE BOOKS WRITTEN AND ILLUSTRATED BY TED LEWIN

Amazon Boy
Fair!
Gorilla Walk (with Betsy Lewin)
Market!
The Reindeer People
Sacred River
The Storytellers
Tiger Trek
When the Rivers Go Home
WORLD WITHIN A WORLD series:
Baja
Everglades
Pribilofs

PICTURE BOOKS ILLUSTRATED BY TED LEWIN:

Ali, Child of the Desert, by Jonathan London
The Always Prayer Shawl, by Sheldon Oberman
American Too, by Elisa Bartone
Bird Watch: A Book of Poetry, by Jane Yolen
Brother Francis and the Friendly Beasts, by Margaret Hodges
Cowboy Country, by Ann H. Scott
The Day of Ahmed's Secret, by Florence Parry Heide
and Judith Heide Gilliland
Faithful Elephants, by Yukio Tsuchiya
The Great Pumpkin Switch, by Meg McDonald
I Wonder if I'll See a Whale, by Franc Weller
Just in Time for Christmas, by Louise Borden
Lost Moose, by Jan Slepian
Matthew's Meadow, by Corinne Demas Bliss
The Originals, by Jane Yolen
Paperboy, by Mary Kroeger and Louise Borden
Peppe the Lamplighter, by Elisa Bartone (a Caldecott Honor Book)
The Potato Man, by Meg McDonald
Sami and the Time of the Troubles, by Florence Parry Heide
and Judith Heide Gilliland
Sea Watch: A Book of Poetry, by Jane Yolen

CONTENTS

A NOTE
FROM THE AUTHOR

This book grew out of an itch I've always had to see the world, an itch I started scratching some thirty years ago. Since then my wife, Betsy, and I have traveled to Australia, India, Nepal, Botswana, Namibia, Kenya, Uganda, Tanzania, Morocco, Egypt, Brazil, Ecuador, the Galápagos Islands, the Caribbean, Ireland, England, France, Germany, Italy, Lapland, Canada, the western United States, Alaska, the Pribilof Islands, and Baja, Mexico. These travels have provided the inspiration for many of my picture books, but often some of my most memorable travel moments my brief acquaintances with people along the way—don't fit into a thirty-two-page picture book story. Here, then, are some of those people, people who have touched me briefly but powerfully before I've had to move on.

TOUCH AND GO

1

MEETING EBONINI
Kalahari Desert, Botswana

"I want you to come to Botswana," said Syd as we stood in my Brooklyn studio looking at paintings I'd done of African wildlife. "I want to take you into the Kalahari and have you meet the Bushmen. I want you to do a book about them." Syd probably knew more about the Bushmen and how to find them in their nomadic wanderings than anyone else in Botswana. He was their good friend, sharing medicine and meat from his hunts and helping them in any way he could.

Six months later I was sitting in a Land Cruiser on the Ghanzi Highway, a soft sand track heading into the Kalahari and back in time. The Land Cruiser slipped and slid, leaving a contrail of dust for miles. Baboons gazed at us, barked, then bounded into the bush.

"What are the Bushmen like?" I asked Syd.

"Charming little chaps," he said. "Still living in the Stone Age."

We drove into darkness, then pitch-blackness. Syd had been driving for hours by then; he seemed hypnotized. Nightjars—

I

nocturnal birds—appeared in the headlight beams like messengers from the underworld. Finally a pinprick of light appeared in the blackness.

"Roger's camp," said Syd. "We'll spend the night. Got to do a little engine work. Don't like the sound of it."

We pulled into a compound of corrugated tin and cinder block huts. Flashlight beams bobbed toward us, with disembodied voices behind them laughing, shouting out greetings. English, Scots, South African accents—the geologists at Roger's camp.

The lights danced about and settled momentarily on a golden, high-cheeked face, crowned by a jackal fur cap. The image took my breath away.

"Who's that?" I asked.

Syd unfolded himself from under the hood, looked, and smiled. "Oh, that's Ebonini, our Bushman tracker. Beautiful, isn't he?"

THE THORN

Kalahari Desert, Botswana

Ebonini sat holding his left foot on his right thigh, a twig in his hand. He was working diligently on the thickly callused sole of his doll-like foot, scraping and digging and probing, apparently to no avail. I asked Syd to find out what he was doing.

Syd obliged and translated the answer. "He's trying to get a thorn out of his foot."

I watched as Ebonini continued to probe, but the twig tool was useless against the leatherlike sole of his foot. On an impulse, I gave him my pocketknife. He half stood up, took the knife, smiled broadly, and nodded. He put the knife in the little plastic bag in which he carried all his valuables—there were already three pocketknives in it. Then he nodded again, sat back down, seemed to forget I was there, and took up where he'd left off, trying to remove the thorn with the twig.

THE HUNTERS
Kalahari Desert, Botswana

"C'mon, man!" Syd shouted. "We'll need help lifting the carcass up on the hunting rig." Syd knew the way I felt about shooting animals: I hated it.

We climbed aboard the Land Cruiser, guns stowed in back, Syd driving, me in the front seat beside him, and Ebbie standing in the back holding on to the roll bar. We swung out onto the rough track, heading toward a large herd of wildebeest we'd seen earlier.

Syd was in a strange, sullen mood. Ebbie scanned the skyline and said something to Syd. Then silence. Only the whine of the motor and the hot sun.

Soon we saw a large herd of wildebeest feeding quietly in the trees. My stomach was tight. I felt like I was going to an execution. Syd sensed it, and I knew it irritated him. We'd had long talks about my squeamishness, and he thought I should know better.

He stopped the Land Cruiser downwind of the herd and jumped out, taking his gun from the back. Ebbie hopped down, alert and quick. They both moved with sharpness and purpose. No movement wasted, no words spoken. I was to stay behind.

With Ebbie in the lead, they crouched down, only their heads showing above the tall grass. In a few moments, they were gone altogether.

I was alone in the back of the rig, leaning on the roll bar. It was immensely hot and silent. The only signs of life—the wildebeest—were now deep in the trees, out of sight. I thought of them, about to be one less.

Then I heard the rifle shot. Just one. Syd was good. I knew that.

Fifteen minutes later, their heads appeared above the shimmering grass. They hopped into the Cruiser without a word. Syd's face was scarlet, flushed from the effort, and he was still edgy. He put the Cruiser into gear, and we headed for the trees. In a few minutes we were at the killing place. The inert carcass of a wildebeest cow lay on her side in the grass, as if she was sleeping.

"I thought she was a bull," said Syd. "Biggest of the bunch. Hard to tell at that distance. When I saw she was a cow, I thought, Damn! I hope she's not lactating."

He leaned over and pulled her teat several times. Nothing. Blood began to pour out of her mouth onto the sand, turning it black.

"Let's get her on the truck."

There was blood everywhere now.

Syd and I lifted her under her flanks, and Ebbie took her head. She was warm and soft. When we had her halfway up, she slipped out of our hands and dropped back onto the sand. She weighed six hundred pounds, according to Syd.

We tried again. Ebbie got her head onto the truck bed, then

joined us in the rear. We pushed hard and she slid on, her horns bumping on the metal.

Syd slammed the tailgate. The wildebeest's back legs stuck out over the top. The truck bed was a pool of thick blood. Her eyes were wide open, and her tongue had flopped out of her mouth.

Back at camp, the carcass was dumped unceremoniously onto the ground under a camelthorn tree. Bushmen almost never see this much meat at one time, and Ebbie moved like lightning now. He gutted the wildebeest, then tied a rope to her back ankle, flung the rope over a stout tree branch ten feet up, and tied it to a winch on the truck. The winch started, and she was lifted by her back leg. As she went up, the contents of her belly slid out onto the sand. Ebbie knelt on the mess, retrieved the stomach, and cut it open. Its yellow-green contents spilled out. He put the stomach in a burlap sack. According to Syd, Bushmen love the stomach.

I started to sketch the procedure, in spite of my squeamishness.

"I wanted you to see one up close," said Syd. "See its color? Beautiful, isn't it?"

It was. Very beautiful. Blue-gray one moment, reddish brown the next, swinging slowly on the rope, its black mane wild and wiry.

The skinning went on until the carcass was naked and looked like a proper side of beef hanging in a butcher shop. I felt more comfortable then. It wasn't real anymore.

Ebbie reduced the carcass even further, to pieces he could lift.

"We'll put these high in the trees so the hyenas won't get them tonight, and we'll make biltong [jerky] tomorrow," said Syd. "Cheer up, man! Let's have a beer."

SYD SNAPS HIS FINGERS
Okavango Delta, Botswana

Syd jammed on the brakes and pointed into the thick bush. Through a tunnel in the cover, I could see a herd of Cape buffalo. One big bull, nose and muzzle dripping, stared at us. A young reddish calf stood near him. Other buffalo appeared through holes in the leaves.

"Any volunteers?" Syd asked.

I looked around; there was no one else but me.

Plunging into the thick, I felt like we were on a suicide mission. The buffalo turned and faded into the bush. We came to a clearing with a big tree in the middle. A good place to leap if need be, I thought.

Syd kneeled and looked under the bushes at ground level, then motioned me to look too. I saw black buffalo legs all over the place.

"The chaps forget they got legs," said Syd. He pointed again. Right in front of us, not forty feet away, three bulls stood like a wall. "It's not those chaps I'm worried about," Syd whispered. "It's the one over there."

I looked over my shoulder and saw black legs below a bush, very close. We were surrounded.

Suddenly Syd snapped his fingers. The buffalo came forward, intrigued, crashing through the bush to stop a few feet from us. We heard grunts and belly roars. He snapped his fingers again. The buffalo stared at us. Syd checked the one on our right and motioned me back to the tree. Then he stood up and turned his back on them like a matador, and we walked nonchalantly through the clearing toward the road.

"Sometimes you can get them to come right toward you by snapping your fingers," Syd said. "Sometimes they run like hell the other way. You see, they're not the killers people make them out to be. I think they're the most noble animals of all."

THE GIVER

Okavango Delta, Botswana

The old Batswana man came into camp bringing a gift of fresh milk, which he carried in a large tin with a makeshift wire handle. On the tin was printed SALAD OIL—PROVIDED BY THE PEOPLE OF THE UNITED STATES OF AMERICA and a stylized drawing of a handshake. Tiny and crinkle-faced, the man wore torn shorts and a worn suit coat. He presented the gift, smiling sweetly and bowing. We accepted it, and he squatted by a nearby tree to watch us.

As he began to understand the camp activity, he leaped up to lend a hand whenever he saw an opportunity. We were in the process of breaking camp, so there was much lifting and rolling of cots and packing of gear. He willingly helped with it all. When we were through, he went to his tree and squatted there again, watching us with bright eyes.

We gave him what was left of our mealie meal, a half-empty bag. Paltry, I thought, compared with his gift of fresh milk. We poured the last of our ice cubes and water into his PEOPLE OF THE UNITED STATES tin. He took it gingerly in his hands, his eyes glowing, and returned to his tree. He put the tin to his lips as if it were a chalice, closed his eyes, and slowly drained it of the cold, sweet water. Then he licked his lips, a look of absolute satisfaction on his face.

The available water around that place was brackish and almost undrinkable. And before he came, we had been planning to pour ours into the sand.

SHEILA
Okavango Delta, Botswana

Third Bridge was, at best, a rickety affair, made of *mopani* poles lashed together with baling wire. Now, with all the rain, it was underwater to boot.

"Just go easy, man," Sheila told Arabang, our Bushman driver, as he eased our big Toyota Hylux truck onto the bridge. Hubcap-deep, we began to bump and sway across. Halfway over, our back tires went through the bridge. We climbed out gingerly. The truck was at a forty-five-degree angle. It looked like it might fall completely through the bridge and sink to the bottom of the river at any second.

Sheila surveyed the situation. "Looks like the last blokes over broke it and didn't bother to repair it. Let's get to it."

I found some logs stacked at the end of the bridge for just this purpose and dragged them out onto the flooded bridge.

"In we go, chaps," said Sheila as she jumped into the waist-deep water.

I jumped in alongside her, and we began to float the logs into place under the back tires. Arabang got the jack out and tried to lift the big truck. Twice it slipped, and the truck lurched back. The rushing water pushed hard against us as we struggled with the floating logs.

"Come on, man," Sheila said to Arabang. "Jump in and give us a hand."

Arabang stuck his hands in his pockets and vehemently shook his head. That seemed really odd to me; he usually did without hesitation anything Sheila asked. Then I noticed a large, freshly painted sign in the middle of the bridge.

DANGER

NO SWIMMING

CROCODILES

My heart leaped into my throat. I looked down around my feet in the clear water, then scanned the riverbanks.

"Come on, man, push!" said Sheila.

"Did you see that sign?" I asked.

"Forget about the sign. There aren't any crocs here. Push!"

Finally we got the logs in place. I attached them with heavy wire, then hauled myself out of the river back onto the bridge and pulled Sheila out next to me. It was late afternoon by then—time to head back to camp.

Arabang started the truck and finished the crossing. We waded behind him to the end of the bridge, got into the truck, and started back across. The rebuilt bridge swayed and creaked, but it held.

Later, back in camp, I told Derek, a bush pilot from Maun, what had happened at Third Bridge.

"Do you know why that sign is there?" he asked—and told me the story. Two weeks before, a villager walking across the bridge before it was underwater knelt down to wash his hands.

A big croc leaped from beneath the surface and swallowed the man's arm up to the shoulder. The man pulled back with all he had, but the croc held on. Its teeth shredded the man's arm all the way down to his hand. Finally he struggled free and managed to get to camp, where someone radioed for a plane. Derek flew his Cessna in and transported him to the little hospital in Maun. The man had been in terrible shape and almost bled to death.

I looked at Sheila. A friend for twenty years, she manages a camp in the Okavango and knows the countryside and its wildlife like the back of her hand.

"You said there were no crocs there," I said.

Sheila chuckled. "How else were we going to get the truck out, man?"

THE HIKERS
Denali National Park, Alaska

I was waiting on the only road through the park for the old school bus now used to pick up hikers like me and take them back to their campsites. It was the last bus of the day, and I didn't want to miss it. In front of me stretched miles of rolling tundra on the verge of autumn. Fourteen miles away, in air so clear they seemed within reach, were the snow-capped peaks of the Alaska Range.

I'd spent the whole day following a rocky glacial streambed all the way to the glacier that created it, then back again, hoping to catch sight of a grizzly. The only wildlife I'd seen were a golden eagle and a lone white wolf.

But now, as I scanned with binoculars, I saw four hikers walking the same streambed. One was wearing a bright red jacket.

Suddenly a big bull caribou came over a rise, heading their way. The hikers were about to cross his path when the caribou got their scent, stopped, then slid down the steep bank and hid behind a rock.

I looked back at the hikers. They were completely unaware, walking four abreast, when the caribou stepped out directly in front of them, looking as big as a moose. The hikers froze, clearly scared to death. Then Red Jacket turned and ran like a jackrabbit. The others dropped their packs and passed *him* as though he was standing still. The caribou, in a rather self-satisfied manner, strutted up the other bank and trotted off.

It was so funny I laughed out loud.

Just then I heard the bus coming and turned around. There, on the other side of the road not fifty feet from me, was a big grizzly bear chomping on a blueberry bush.

THE GOOD SAMARITAN
Churchill, Manitoba, Canada

"The best place to find them is at the town dump," the man said. He was standing in front of a big Quonset hut with a sign on the door that read BEAR JAIL—NO TRESPASSING. All around were enormous sections of pipe with bars on the ends, mounted on flatbed trailers. These were used to capture and carry off to jail any bears that came into town and got into trouble. As soon as Hudson Bay froze, the bears would be set free to go about their business on the sea ice.

"Just go down to the dump. There's always some bears there."

It wasn't the setting I had in mind, but dump bears were better than no bears, so I took his advice.

I was about to turn onto the road to the dump when something white caught my eye. On the shore of the bay was a big—*really* big—polar bear. He stood for only a second, then lay back down in the brilliant red fireweed.

I pulled my van off the road and promptly got stuck in the

sand. I got out to look over the situation. The sleeping bear lay almost hidden, a hundred yards away.

A car stopped on the road, and a local woman got out. "Can I help?" she asked.

"Yes, I'm stuck," I replied.

She put a piece of wood (carried for just such a purpose) under my back tires, and I got ready to back out over it.

"Why did you pull off the road anyway?" she asked then.

"To get a better look at that polar bear over there," I told her, pointing.

"Oh, my God!" she gasped, then shoved me over, jumped in, slammed the door, and stomped on the accelerator. We lurched back onto the road. The bear looked up for a moment, then fell back into a torpor.

The woman gave me an icy glare. *"Don't ever do that again!"*

As she got into her own car, she added, "You know, when you live up here, anything that's white and moves scares you half to death. Even when I'm on vacation in the city, if someone passes near me wearing a white coat, I jump right out of my skin."

ORVILLE BIG LEGS
Northwest Territories, Canada

I had a fifty-gallon drum of gasoline sloshing around in the back of the old station wagon as I arrived at Orville's village. It was all arranged—all I had to do was bring the gas. Orville had an aluminum skiff with an outboard motor, but no gas.

Orville Grand Jambe, or Orville Big Legs in English, a thin young Cree with intense black eyes, was waiting for me. He siphoned the gas into small jerricans and loaded them into the boat tied at the foot of a steep bank. I got in and Orville jumped deftly in behind me, carrying a battered old Winchester, its stock held together with silver duct tape. He stashed it in the back by the motor, and we swung out into the brown river.

I pointed at the camera slung around my neck and told him I wanted to photograph bears. He nodded, but I wasn't sure he understood. We plowed upstream in the middle of the river, which was almost a mile wide at that point. Suddenly Orville swung the bow toward the left bank. I looked at the tree line but saw nothing.

We were closing quickly on the shore when I saw a yearling

black bear stick its head and shoulders out of the forest. I lifted my camera. Orville had understood after all, I thought. I focused and the bear came sharply into view.

BAM!

The bear disappeared.

My ears were ringing painfully as I turned around. There was Orville, standing up in the speeding boat. He had just shot the bear right over my head.

The skiff slammed into the bank. Orville, hard-eyed, gun in hand, leaped over me and out of the skiff. Sliding and falling, he ran up the steep bank, gained the crest, and disappeared into the forest.

Through the ringing in my ears I heard crashing and dragging sounds in the woods. Maybe the bear is killing him, I thought.

I climbed the bank and stood tentatively at the edge of the woods. There was Orville, covered with blood. He was dressing out the bear.

He showed me the bullet wound, right through the heart.

Amazing! I thought. Standing up in a moving boat from a hundred yards with a broken Winchester!

Working expertly, Orville severed the head, put a slit in the upper lip, and hung the head on a sapling where it would be visible from the river. He would pick up the carcass on his way home. He turned it over and covered it with branches, then wiped off his knife, sheathed it, picked up his broken Winchester, and quickly slid down the bank.

I looked down at the half-hidden corpse, then up at its head dangling by the lip out over the Peace River. Then I walked slowly back to the skiff, my camera still slung around my neck.

Orville shot at three more bears that day. He missed two, shot one in the foot, and never saw a fourth. I saw it—a big cinnamon bear—but I kept it to myself.

10

CAPTAIN NAPOLEON
Galápagos Islands

She sat, dead in the water, *Jesus del Gran Poder* (Jesus Is Mighty)—or, more simply, *The Poderoso*—listing slightly to port, stinking of diesel oil and insect spray, and without a captain. Her last captain, Napoleon, had to have her towed all the way from Hood Island. He'd had enough.

I'd known yesterday that something was wrong when he'd knelt in front of a little shrine in the cantina on shore, lit a candle, and crossed himself several times. He hadn't looked happy.

That night he was crammed into the pitch-black bowels of the ship, hammering and banging on its diesel engine. Nilo, the ship's cook, held a flashlight. I sat in the stern, watching by candlelight. Once they tried to turn the engine over, but it coughed and died. On Nilo's portable radio, a chorus of children repeated over and over, "*Dios te Salve Maria lleva es tu gracia* [Hail Mary, full of grace]."

The captain finally left with Nilo and went ashore to get drunk. Nilo rowed back at midnight to tell me there would be a new captain in the morning.

Captain Fausto smiled reassuringly at me as he stepped aboard with a new battery. That evening the generator hummed, and Nilo baked a cake.

NILO AND THE RADIO
Galápagos Islands

Nilo took his radio apart to fix it. Carefully removing all the screws, he laid them on the deck, then took out the innards and rearranged them.

When he got it all back together, it played only static. He sat the whole evening with his arm around it, desolate, like he'd lost his best friend.

The next day it was playing fine. I think he fixed it with a meat cleaver.

12

MARGRET'S TORTOISES

Floreana Island, Galápagos

In 1950 Margret Wittmer, the longtime postmistress on Floreana, hired some local people to collect giant tortoises to sell to a woman from the Los Angeles zoo. They collected eight tiny young tortoises.

Margret wrote to the zoo woman, telling her the tortoises were ready. The woman's husband responded, saying that she was in India.

On the way home, while passing through the Panama Canal, the zoo woman died of a disease she had contracted in India.

Marget Wittmer still has the tortoises. They live in a lava-stone corral in her backyard. The tortoises now weigh over two hundred pounds each. Her chickens feed in among them.

THE DIRECTOR
San Cristóbal, Galápagos

The sign next to the big wooden doors read San Cristóbal Museum. Inside, an Indian woman sat in Rembrandt light, holding a small, fat-faced child in a pink pointed cap. Before her was a black table with a small Ecuadorean flag on a pedestal; behind her, an old wooden bookcase. Holding the child facedown over one bent arm, she motioned with her free hand for me to come inside.

At the far end of a big gloomy room with a low wooden ceiling was a high-ceilinged gallery and a balcony full of glass display cases. Daylight spilled down from the gallery windows, illuminating a collection of cattle and goat skulls with horns, all alien to these islands. Next to them was an assortment of sperm whale ribs, arranged artfully around a section of whale vertebrae. A post in the center of the room held a pilot whale's entire backbone. It looked like a giant drill bit.

Above a collection of stuffed birds, including masked and blue-footed boobies, frigate birds, and long-tailed tropic birds, was a brown pelican with its bill open and its wings outstretched.

All were perched atop skeletons of large cactuses.

In the center of the room, mounted on a small island of volcanic rock and coral, were a porpoise, a Galapagos fur seal with pup, a sea lion, an oddly shaped pilot whale, Sally Lightfoots and various other crabs, a penguin, and a spiny lobster.

And on the last wall, there was an exhibit dedicated to "the Honorable Director" of the museum. A yellowed newspaper clipping showed him at his desk. A series of old black-and-white snapshots showed the white-haired gentleman hard at work preparing specimens—sea urchins, sea horses, the pelican with outstretched wings—and posing with his arm around the stuffed fur seal. The last two photos showed the director embalmed in his casket, his hands folded peacefully on his chest. He had finally become part of the collection himself.

14

THE BERBER AND HIS DONKEY

Rissani, Morocco

Inside the mud-walled ruins of the Ksar Abbar in Rissani, an old Berber man in a dazzling white turban and djellaba, or caftan, was saddling his donkey. I watched each step carefully; he ignored me just as carefully.

I asked my Arab guide, Brahim, if it was all right to photograph him.

"Sure," he said, offering the man up with a sweep of his hands.

The man covered the donkey with a blanket, then threw a thick, padded saddle over that. As far as he was concerned, I wasn't there. He paid no attention at all to my camera clicking and whirring as I caught each step of the procedure.

Over the saddle went the shuare, the woven saddlebags. Then the old man stepped onto a low wall and mounted the donkey, both his feet to one side. Still ignoring me completely, he turned the donkey's head with the pressure from a short stick. Then, with a light kick from the man's heels, the donkey trotted off. The old man, his chin held high, bounced along on the donkey's back. As he rode off, he threw Berber words over his shoulder at me.

Brahim began to laugh uncontrollably.

"What did he say?" I asked

"'Take a thousand pictures. I don't care!'"

THE BLUE MAN

Marrakech, Morocco

By evening, the square at the entrance to the old walled city of Marrakech was jammed with Berber musicians from the High Atlas Mountains, acrobats, dancers, snake charmers, even dentists. Jugglers threw their antique fusils (muskets) thirty feet into the air. A storyteller sat cross-legged on the ground, his tiny granddaughter beside him with a white dove atop her head. The dove was sent high into the air to bring back a story from the sky. Rose water men, dressed like fools in a medieval court, moved through the crowds ringing bells, their wide-brimmed hats jingling with bells of their own. The smells of simmering pots of *harira,* couscous, fish, and meat cooking on smoky charcoal grills filled the night air.

The square was called Djemma el Fna, the Place of the Dead. Here, where a thousand years ago the heads of executed criminals were displayed on pikes, the "blue man" sat on an Oriental rug. A Tuareg, he wore the indigo robes of his people, which stained his skin blue. Beside him was a battered old leather portmanteau. Surrounding him were rows of glass jars and plastic boxes filled with folk remedies, a small balance scale, necklaces of amber, huge python skins rolled and neatly tied, brass incense burners, and an ostrich egg. His lantern cast deep shadows, and his eyes glowed like charcoal embers as he stared intently at the crowd. He had placed his left foot behind his neck, and in his right hand he held a photo of a dead sperm whale.

The crowd stared back at him, spellbound. The lantern hissed.

THE HOLY BOY

Dakshin Kali, Nepal

"Pleeeeze, pleeeeeze," whined the wizened old crone, extending her cupped hands. She stayed right with me as I started down the ancient stone steps to the temple dedicated to Kali, the goddess of wrath. "Pleeeeeze, pleeeeeze." As soon as I left her territory, she waved me off in contempt, making a horrible face at me.

Next in line was a crippled beggar lying on the ground. As I stepped into his territory, his withered limbs began to quiver like a wounded seal.

The gauntlet of beggars continued until I reached the bottom of the steps, where a small stone bridge crossed a stream. It was jammed with pilgrims, many with young goats strapped to the bundles they carried on their backs.

The pilgrims brought their goats into a courtyard behind the temple, where they handed the frightened creatures to a man with a long-bladed knife. The floor and walls of the courtyard were awash with blood. The man placed each goat between his knees, pulled its head back to expose its throat, then proceeded to saw away with the knife until he severed the jugular.

Each pilgrim then handed the man a few coins, put his palms together prayerfully, bowed, and carried off his dead goat. The sacrifice of the animals is a hardship for these poor people, who would reap more benefit from a live goat's milk, but once the goat is dead, the sacrifice has been made. The pilgrims carried their dead goats back to the stream bank, skinned them, cooked them, and ate them.

At the temple entrance there was a crush of people, all carrying *jai* flowers in offering. The air was a smoky haze from burning incense.

In a small dark room inside the temple sat a young boy with a painted face—a holy boy. He was dressed in white and wore a turban the color of burnished gold. He was surrounded by holy objects: *jai* flowers, dishes of dry pigment, brass prayer bowls, sticks of burning incense. He sat cross-legged with his upturned palms in his lap. The colors and textures surrounding him, the smoke and smell of the incense, the gonging of the temple bells, and the nervous, insistent bleating of the goats outside made the boy appear, momentarily, to float.

17

TALAT

Aswan, Egypt

"I am Talat," said the lean, elegant Nubian, "and this is our driver." He gestured toward a small dark man in a turban and flowing galabia (the Egyptian word for a caftan). They had met me at the airport in Aswan to take me to the *Nile Princess,* an enormous floating hotel, for a five-day trip on the Nile.

As we drove through the crowded streets of Aswan, Talat leaned over the backseat to talk. "How are you enjoying Egypt?" he asked.

I told him of my travels so far and how I'd especially enjoyed the camel market outside Cairo.

"Ah, you are interested in camels. We have the best camel market in Egypt right here near Aswan. There are many more camels than in Cairo. It is a wonderful thing. Would you like to see it?"

"Yes, absolutely," I said.

"Unfortunately, it is only on Tuesday," he said.

"This *is* Tuesday," I told him.

"Ah, yes. Then we'll arrange it."

Talat and the driver placed my gear on the dock at the foot of the gangplank, and we boarded the *Nile Princess*. I checked in at the desk and surrendered my passport. Then Talat drew me aside.

"I will see if there is time enough to go to the market before your boat sails," he told me. "It is some distance away."

I watched him talking to the desk clerk, who was busily checking in other passengers. The desk clerk shook his head no. Talat talked more. The clerk shook his head even more vigorously.

Talat came back to me. "Okay, there is time. But we must go now." He quoted me an outlandish price for the trip. "There is no time to bargain. If you wish to go, it must be now."

"Let's do it," I said.

We went back down the gangplank, past my gear sitting alone on the dock, and up to the car. The driver got in, and Talat held open the back door for me. I got in, and he closed the door.

"The driver will take you. He knows where it is. You can pay me later. Go now."

A few minutes later we were in the desert heading toward the Sudan border.

"Where is the market?" I asked the driver.

He looked at me in the rearview mirror and smiled.

"Will we have enough time to get there and back before the boat sails?" I asked.

This time he turned around and smiled.

Up ahead was a checkpoint with a barrier and several heavily

33

armed soldiers. I automatically reached for my passport, then remembered with a sinking feeling that it was on the boat.

The driver stopped. A soldier with a machine gun strode over, bent down, and stared at me. The driver said something to him under his breath and slipped him some money. The soldier continued to stare. I began to sweat. Finally he stood up, took a step back, and motioned for us to pass. The barrier lifted, and I began to breathe again.

The driver turned around and smiled again. "No problem," he said.

I pointed at my watch and back toward the town.

"No problem," he repeated.

Nubian villages flew by, but no camel market. Time was beginning to worry me. I could see the boat leaving without me, my gear still sitting on the dock.

Finally the little town of Daraw appeared in front of us, crowded with camels—so many camels that we could not move. Camels in front of us, camels behind us, camels filling every street and alley. We moved at a camel's pace along with them until we spilled out into a great open space surrounded by date palms. It was jam-packed with camels and their Sudanese drivers. The men, some in black, others in faded pastel galabias and turbans, were herding the beasts by beating them with big sticks. The camels were hobbled, one front leg bent at the knee and tied, which caused them to move with an odd, three-legged gait, kicking sand into clouds of fine dust.

Some of the men lounged on reed mats under makeshift tents, smoking nargilehs (water pipes) and sipping tea.

An old Sudanese man came up to me and shook my hand. "Where are you from?" he asked, in English.

"America," I said.

"Why don't you buy a camel?" he asked, gesturing at the wonderful bargains all around us.

"Where would I put it?" I said, laughing.

"On your front porch," he answered very seriously.

My driver tapped me on the shoulder and pointed at his watch. I looked at mine—by my calculations, we could not possibly make it back to the boat on time. It had taken over an hour to get here, and we had less than an hour to get back. Now, to drive out of town, we had to go against the flow of camels pouring into the marketplace.

Inch by inch we moved through town, the clock ticking. Finally we were on the main road again. In just thirty-five minutes, we were at dockside.

"No problem," said the driver.

My gear had been safely stowed on board, and there was Talat, waiting on the gangplank. "How did you enjoy it?" he asked as I gave him his money.

"It was fantastic," I said.

"Ah, good," he said. "I myself have never been there."

THE PET SELLER

Cairo, Egypt

A stack of wooden cages held hedgehogs, jerboas (jumping mice), three different kinds of lizards, several falcons, and a dozen bats. A downy yellow chick peeped loudly from a cage it shared with a large owl. The chick was hiding under the breast feathers of the owl, oddly seeking protection from the one who would eventually eat it. Above the cages hung stuffed versions of the live creatures below and the head of a mongoose.

A turbaned man stood behind aquariums of snakes, surrounded by several stuffed hooding cobras. "Welcome to Egypt." He smiled, then reached into an aquarium and lifted out a six-foot cobra. Holding it by the tip of its tail, he stretched it from tail to head several times as if to remove the kinks. Then he placed it on the ground, still holding it by the tail. The snake, more alert now, tried to crawl away. With his free hand, the man stroked its tail against the grain of its scales. The snake whirled around and reared up. The man squatted down and flapped the bottom of his galabia. The snake hooded and struck, hitting only cloth.

BOTSWANA: Cape buffalo

BOTSWANA: Disaster at Third Bridge! Sheila is hanging over the sign, I'm in the water, and Arabang, our driver, is standing by the vehicle.

BOTSWANA: Syd

BOTSWANA: Ebonini

ALASKA: Mount McKinley, Denali National Park

CANADA: Bear trap

CANADA: Orville Grand Jambe (Orville Big Legs) with his Winchester

GALÁPAGOS ISLANDS: *The Poderoso*

GALÁPAGOS ISLANDS: Nilo, the cook

1

2

3

4

5

6

MOROCCO: Berber man saddling his donkey

MOROCCO: With my Tuareg guide

EGYPT: Sudanese camel drivers

EGYPT: Sudanese camel drivers

EGYPT: Sudanese man smoking a nargileh (water pipe)

NORWAY: *Lavu* at Sami winter camp, with aurora borealis in the sky above

INDIA: Prasad and his old friend

INDIA: The Mastagudi
Male, with new teeth

BRAZIL: The macaw man at the Ariau River tower

BRAZIL: Boy with his three-toed
sloth, along the Amazon River

BRAZIL: With a boa constrictor

BRAZIL: *Garimpeiro* boy panning for gold

UNITED STATES: Rex Roberts: An American Cowboy

AUSTRALIA: Aboriginal boy

His partner brought him another snake, and the pet seller got them to hood and strike simultaneously. Then, placing the cobras back in their aquarium, he reached inside another and pulled out a fistful of small vipers. They squeezed out between his fingers. His hand looked like the head of Medusa.

Seeking to impress me further, the pet seller brought out a large plastic jug and removed the lid. Inside were hundreds of ghostly white scorpions. He picked one out and placed it in his hand, pointing to the tiny but terrifying stinger at the end of its curled tail, then returned it to the jug and gestured for me to wait.

Reaching under a stack of cages, he pulled out another plastic jug. Centipedes, orange and black, three inches long, hundreds of them. He dumped a pile into his hand, where they crawled all over each other and up his wrist; then he smiled at me, waiting expectantly for my approval.

"Very nice, " I said.

19
THE MOST AMAZING FACE
Sydney, Australia

There's an old section of Sydney, down by the water, called The Rocks. Tucked away in one of its buildings is the Aboriginal Museum. Inside are Aboriginal paintings, objets d'art, and displays of dwellings and campsites complete with native vegetation, dugouts, throwing sticks, and spears. The displays are as carefully put together as they would be in any natural history museum, but without the usual models of the people who would have inhabited these campsites.

I was wondering about this when I noticed the figure of an Aboriginal person standing in the shadows. I walked over to examine it more closely.

"G'day, mate," it said, stepping forward and almost stopping my heart.

She was a slight young woman about twenty years old, with long amber-colored hair and a face like none other I'd ever seen, anywhere: blue-black, with a large flat nose and a prominent brow ridge that set her eyes back into deep black shadow. A beautiful face that spoke of ancient times, when faces such as this one crossed the land bridge from Asia and spread out across the Australian continent to the eastern shore. The faces of people whose world changed forever with the coming of the white man.

This particular face belonged to the caretaker of a museum of Aboriginal art, campsites, and rough dwellings—but no people.

SPEAKING ENGLISH
Northern Territory, Australia

Halfway to Yellow Water or halfway to Darwin, depending on which way you're going, is the Bark Hut Inn. Outside there's a covered beer garden. Inside there are half a dozen stuffed buffalo heads, several bullwhips, a scattering of worn-out saddles and saddlebags, a stuffed wild boar's head, a massive crocodile skull, a NO SWIMMING—CROCS sign, glass cases full of rifle and artillery shells, one World War I machine gun, one World War II machine gun, some vintage guns on horn racks, any number of hunting arrows, some powder horns, a didgeridoo, some log tables and chairs, some pool tables, and an old fat yellow dog.

There are two signs on the wall:

THE BARK HUT SPECIAL:	
2-LITRE DARWIN STUBBIE	BARK HUT STICKER
DECK OF CARDS	PLUS THE CARRY BAG
BAR TOWELING	ALL FOR ONLY $17.00

```
┌─────────────────────────────────────┐
│              MENU:                    │
│           BULL $8.50                  │
│           BARA $8.50                  │
│        BULL AND BARA $8.50            │
│      BURGER WITH THE LOT $2.50        │
└─────────────────────────────────────┘
```

"I'll have a draft beer," I said.

"Do you want handles?" asked the hefty young woman with blond pigtails behind the counter.

"Handles?"

"What do you call them in America?" She lifted a mug.

"Oh, *mugs*," I said stupidly.

"So you Yanks really like our Hoags," she said, handing me my beer.

"Hoags?" I was beginning to feel really dense.

"Paul Hogan. Crocodile Dundee. You know, some Aussies like to put on airs and pretend they're Brits, but he's a real ocker."

I didn't even ask.

21

A TEACHER TO BE STOPPED

Cooinda, Australia

A van, covered with red mud, pulled up to the little café in Cooinda. It had really done some traveling, all the way from the school in Oenpelli in Arnhem Land, about seventy-five miles away as the crow flies, over very rugged country. A young white man got out, slid the door back, and a gang of Aboriginal kids jumped out and ran into the café. The driver, seeing me standing there with my camera and brand-new didgeridoo (I had just bought it in the café), yelled at the kids to come back.

"This guy has come halfway around the world to see Aboriginals," he said to them. "Come on over here and let him have a look."

I flushed and stammered, "It's okay, really."

"Go ahead, take some pictures," said the teacher.

"No, really, it's fine," I said.

"I see you got a didgeridoo. John, come over here," he said.

A light-skinned, blond Aboriginal boy reluctantly came over. He was painfully shy.

The teacher took the didgeridoo from me. "Here, John, play it for him. He's come all this way to hear it."

There was no stopping the teacher. I felt terrible for the boy. He took the didgeridoo and blew into the end of it. No sound came out. The other kids laughed hysterically at him. He tried again. Nothing.

There was just no stopping the teacher. "Come on, John. You know how," he said.

I took the didgeridoo from the boy. "It's okay," I said. "Thanks for trying."

The boy looked up at me with amazing iridescent amber eyes as he gratefully backed away.

STRANGER IN THE NIGHT

Norway, Sami Winter Camp, 125 Miles above the Arctic Circle

Ola made it look so easy. He just knelt there on the reindeer hides, broke tiny bits of birch twigs, and fed them to the fire, which burned clean and hot and without smoke. Inside the *lavu* (tepee), the temperature was thirty-two degrees Fahrenheit. Outside it had dropped to thirty below.

Ola nurtured the hot, smokeless fire all through coffee and a big pot of *bidus* (reindeer stew), then half stood and swung the low door flap back. Cold came in like the edge of an ax. He pointed at the fire, the kindling beside it, the pile of small birch logs outside, an ax imbedded in one of them, and said something in Sami. I didn't understand the words, but the look on his face was clear: Don't let it go out! He slipped through the opening and closed the flap behind him. Heat filled the *lavu* again.

I heard his snowmobile leave and pulled the reindeer skins up around me. Beneath me, birch branches were covered with more layers of reindeer skins. Some were untanned, and their blood began to seep through my down coveralls. My boots, made of the skins of reindeer heads, curled at the toe where the nose had been. They were stuffed with dried grass.

As darkness fell, the cold outside became even more intense, and the inside of the *lavu* began to feel like an icebox. I slid a small birch log onto the fire. It began to smoke. I tossed in more kindling; it became hotter and smokier. Dark clouds filled the *lavu* and poured out its open top into the frigid night.

I lifted the door flap a few inches to vent the smoke. The temperature inside dropped, and the smoke only got thicker. My eyes burned. The part of me facing the fire was hot, the part of me facing away was freezing, and I was choking.

As I struggled with the fire, I heard a snowmobile getting closer and closer until it stopped in front of the *lavu*. The tent flap flew open. A short, squat Sami man stood there, framed by the cold night sky. The firelight played on him, and the smoke enveloped him. He looked like Vulcan.

Coughing violently, he grabbed the tent flap and snapped it back and forth several times. The smoke disappeared. Then he stepped in, closed the flap, and knelt. He picked up some twigs, broke them, and fed them to the fire. Once again it burned low, clean, and hot.

The man said nothing, just stared into the flames. It was two o'clock in the morning. I offered him some coffee from the fire-blackened pot in the embers. He took it, warmed his hands on the cup, and swigged it down. Then, backing up on his knees, he opened the flap door and crouched out into the bitter cold. The flap slapped shut. I heard his motor cough to life and he roared off. I looked down at the fire. It snapped and crackled and warmed the *lavu* without a bit of smoke.

PRASAD

Nagarhole National Park, India

Prasad beat his temples with his fists and knelt down next to the dead tiger. "I am totally upset," he said.

I placed my hand on the tiger's chest and ran it over the thick, hard muscles of its shoulder. It was still warm. One of its canine teeth was broken; the other was longer than my thumb. It had no right eye at all. Ten feet long to the tip of its tail, it weighed about four hundred pounds. Its right paw and foreleg were grotesquely swollen from a deep wound. Prasad said the flies and maggots had finally killed it. They'd done what the other big male he'd fought with could not.

He was called the Mastagudi Male, Prasad told me, named for this part of the jungle. There were many stories about him—like the time he'd been lying in the mud to keep cool. When he emerged from the bamboo thicket, his stripes had disappeared under the mud; even his long whiskers were coated with it. The villagers thought he was a demon.

He'd been seen swimming across the wide Kabini River many times. A few years ago, he was seen limping from a wound suffered in another battle. He'd licked it and cured himself that time.

"Only the other day, I saw him playing with a big elephant," said Prasad. "The tusker chased him away, lowering his head so that his tusks made two furrows in the ground."

Prasad lay down alongside the dead tiger and put his arm over its chest. "Please take a picture of me and my old friend."

Postscript: The Mastagudi Male is now stuffed and mounted and resides in the office of the Deputy Conservator of Forests, in a little town near Nagarhole called Uncel. The taxidermist has given him two good eyes and four good canine teeth. Soon he will go back home to Nagarhole where he will be placed in a glass case in the great hall of the Kabini River Lodge—protected in death as he never was in life.

THE KING OF RANTHAMBOR

Sawai Madhopur, India

There was a curtain in lieu of a door, behind which I could hear wild Indian music. The small man I was with folded his hands prayerfully in front of his face, bowed slightly, then parted the curtain, and the music hit me full in the face.

The room was spare and cool. A mattress beneath a white sheet covered the entire floor. Two enormous speakers filled one wall. The only other furniture was a cabinet next to the mattress. On it was a framed eight-by-ten photograph of a beautiful Western woman looking vaguely like an American movie star.

Sitting cross-legged on the mattress was a small, lean man with a carefully groomed handlebar mustache. He was dressed in an exquisitely pressed military-style shirt, a mauve ascot, and thick tinted glasses. He had gutted a small transistor radio, and its insides were strewn all over the white sheet like intestines.

He looked up. "Yes? What is it?"

"I have a letter from Rekwar."

"Leave your shoes there and sit." He motioned me to sit on the mattress.

I noticed he had *his* shoes on, but I took mine off and sat cross-legged next to him.

"Well?"

I handed him the letter. The music continued to blare as he read.

My eyes fell on the radio's intestines. When I looked up, my eyes met his—sharp behind the thick lenses.

"First rule: Save all the parts," I said.

He looked at the radio and chuckled. "Okay, what can I do for you?"

"I need a Jeep, and I'd like to stay at Jogi Mahal." Jogi Mahal is an old maharaja's palace in Ranthambor National Park.

He knew this, of course, from Rekwar's letter. Rekwar had said that this man was king of Ranthambor, so nothing would be a problem. It wasn't.

"Done. What did Rekwar charge you for his Jeep?" he asked.

"Four hundred fifty rupees, plus the driver."

"We can do a little better." He smiled.

He looked up at the small brown man still holding the curtain back and nodded. All was understood.

"I'll call the garage man myself and make sure the Jeep is ready or it'll never arrive. You can meanwhile go to the market."

"Will I need food or . . ."

He waved off the question. "No. We have everything at Jogi Mahal."

Then he turned back to his disemboweled radio and immediately got lost in it.

The man at the curtain motioned for me to follow. I put my shoes back on and left Fateh Singh, the king of Ranthambor, to his radio.

25
THE MAHOUT
Kanha National Park, India

The mahout sat on the elephant's neck, wrapped in nondescript rags like a beggar. He held a short, thick stick in his right hand and a little dark cigarette called a *bidi* in his left. Smoke came out from under his rag hood each time he exhaled.

I sat fourteen feet above the ground in a wooden howdah behind the mahout, my feet dangling over one side, a wooden railing holding me secure. The howdah creaked and rocked gently with the rolling gait of the huge creature beneath us. Hard and hairy, sweet-smelling like a draft horse, she sighed and blew as she went.

The elephant stopped to drink from a little stream. The mahout screamed at her in Hindi and kicked her behind the ear, where a vein the size of my thumb was very near the surface. Then he kicked her simultaneously with both his bare feet. He wanted her to move forward, but she just continued to drink.

Screaming louder, he raised his stick high in the air and brought it down so hard on her forehead that it lifted him right up off her neck. Dust rose from her forehead as the stick slammed down, but the elephant didn't budge.

The mahout hit her again with such force that the stick flipped out of his hand and fell into the stream. The elephant winced and made a pathetically small groan.

Not wanting to climb down in tiger country to retrieve the stick, the mahout asked the elephant in a soft, sweet, singsong voice to pick up the stick and hand it to him. The elephant shifted from one foot to the other, as if trying to decide whether she should give the fly on her back the ability to sting her again.

The mahout's song went on. Embracing the elephant's huge neck, he sang in her ear in a most seductive way. Finally the elephant, having drunk her fill, found the stick with her trunk and deftly picked it up. Holding it at trunk's length, she dangled it in front of the mahout like a carrot. He climbed out on her head and stretched as far as he could, but he still couldn't reach it. Finally, tiring of the game, the elephant curled her trunk back and handed it to him.

The battle of wills was over. Gently now, the mahout urged his elephant forward with his toes toward the dark wall of jungle ahead.

SOMETHING SPECIAL

Banaras, India

The little boy talked incessantly. The old boatman had picked him up an hour earlier on the ghats (stone steps) among the bathing pilgrims, and he'd been talking ever since. The boatman put his back into the oars and we creaked up the Ganges as the sun rose over the old palaces and temples above the ghats. The kid kept right on talking. Though he spoke in English, I couldn't make out a single word as he babbled on.

The boatman finally put us ashore, and I followed the boy up the slippery ghats to the narrow, winding streets above. He was still talking. I made out the words "something special," but nothing more.

The boy led me down dark streets that were no more than cracks between the buildings. The smell of human waste was overpowering. We passed pilgrims crushing into the Golden Temple behind a high wall. "Something special," he said again, and gestured for me to follow him further.

Finally we came to a crumbling old building and entered. The dark, dank stairs circled up around a hollow space in the center, like an elevator shaft without the elevator. The boy pointed in the direction of the Ganges, then at the shaft. I understood. It was a giant drainpipe. When the river flooded, water rose up in the building; when the river receded, the water drained out through the shaft.

There were rooms on each landing, concealed by curtains. On the top floor, the boy led me to a curtained doorway and said, "My father, something special." He pulled the fabric aside. Inside, a man in a long Indian tunic pointed at my shoes. I took them off. He gestured for me to sit on the floor. The boy hovered in a corner, looking apprehensive.

I looked around the tiny room. It was furnished only with a sleeping platform and an old battered locker.

"I want to show you something," said the man, removing a large stack of embroidered silk panels from the locker. The boy smiled encouragingly, looking all the while at my hand-tooled leather belt with the antique Navajo silver buckle.

"I will go through them one by one," said his father. "Tell me to stop when you see one you like."

He started through the embroidered panels, lifting one off, then laying it aside, exposing the next one. They were awful. At each, he looked at me for a sign. I gave none. At last he got to the end. He looked at me intently. I hadn't said a word. They were all awful.

The boy now began to look frightened.

"I will go through them one by one," his father said again. "Tell me to stop when you see one you like." And slowly, one by one, he went through them all again, looking each time for any minute reaction from me. I didn't even blink.

When he got to the last one, he glared at the boy, then got up and went to the locker. As he reached inside, his back to me, he said, "My father made this one; it is something special."

53

Then he turned with a flourish, holding the largest and most awful one yet. His eyes burned into me, looking for any sign of weakening. I remained inscrutable, though I did glance at my shoes near the doorway.

Finally I said, "No, thank you. I really must go." I got up and put on my shoes.

He folded the cloth carefully, shaking his head from side to side. "Eastern ways," he said, and then, with much disgust, "Western ways."

I stepped out into the dark stairwell. A moment later I heard a terrible scream from behind the curtain. When the boy came out, he was crying.

I followed him down the stairs and out into the dark maze of streets. Except for an occasional, tearful sniffle, the boy was silent.

When we came at last to the bright square in the center of town, I offered him some money.

He shook his head no, looked at my waist, and said, "I want your belt."

THE MONEY CHANGERS
Cuiabá, Mato Grosso, Brazil

The phone rang in my hotel room. *Who* in this little cow town on the edge of the Pantanal in western Brazil would be calling *me?* I wondered. I picked up the phone and the person on the other end spoke to me in Portuguese. Since I don't speak a single word of Portuguese, I hung up and went down to the lobby. There at the desk phone were two Lebanese men. One of them wrote on a slip of paper and handed it to me: "100C [*Cruzados*]=$1."

The men were illegal money changers. I hadn't asked for them, but they seemed to be able to smell that I needed cash. I was heading into the Pantanal—a freshwater marsh about the size of Pennsylvania—the next day, and only cash will do in the bush.

I shook my head no and wrote "150C=$1." The man took the slip, looked me hard in the eye, looked at his partner, then wrote "110C=$1." I wrote "150C=$1" again. When I handed him the slip, he reached into his pockets and pulled them inside out. I was picking his pocket, he was telling me.

Slowly and deliberately, he wrote "120C=$1" and underlined it. I wrote, just as deliberately, "140C=$1" and underlined *it*. He moaned and he and his partner stepped aside for a conference. When they came back, he wrote "130C=$1" and picked up their briefcase, ready to walk. I moaned, looking unhappy, but nodded yes. I wrote down "$1,000" and he nodded. He pointed at the calendar on the hotel desk, and I understood they would be back at the same time the next day.

This time I was waiting for their phone call, but I jumped all the same when it came. I met them at the desk. They had a huge suitcase with them, and they were very nervous, looking behind them constantly. We sat down in a corner of the lobby. Through the big front windows, I noticed a car standing with its motor running. They opened the suitcase partway. It was full of money, like a ransom. One of the men nervously said something to the other, slammed the suitcase shut, and gestured toward the elevator. We all got on and went to my room. There they relaxed a bit, opened the suitcase, and dumped the money in a big pile on the bed. They showed me the slip from the day before, "130C=$1," and nodded. I counted out ten neatly folded one-hundred-dollar bills from my money belt with the hidden zipper, and handed the money to them. They gestured at the pile on the bed. "Count it," the gesture said, and they sat down to wait. I shook my head—"It's okay."—and tried to show them out. They wouldn't budge, and they pointed at the money. I sat on the edge of the bed and began to count. One . . . two . . . three . . . four . . . . An hour and a half later—one hundred twenty-nine thousand, nine hundred ninety-nine . . . one hundred thirty thousand. They got up, went to the door, shook my hand, and then, looking both ways in the hall, slipped into the elevator.

I watched from my window as they ran out the front door of the hotel, leaped into the car with the motor running, and sped off. I turned around to the pile of *cruzados* now in neat stacks on my bed and thought, How, exactly, am I going to get that into my money belt with the hidden zipper?

MACAW MAN

Ariau River Lodge, Amazonas, Brazil

In the middle of the Amazon rain forest, on the Ariau River, there's a tower you can climb to watch flocks of macaws fly above the treetops at sunrise. An old man there takes care of resident and orphaned animals that hang around the place. Ten big scarlet macaws fight for the chance to sit on his head.

There's a tiny squirrel monkey, spoiled rotten, and a small green parrot. The monkey absolutely hates that parrot. One morning I heard terrible screaming. The monkey had the parrot by the throat with both hands and was choking it to death. The old man jumped in and broke it up. Then he motioned for me to follow him.

We left the tower, followed by the squirrel monkey, and crossed a series of elevated walkways through the jungle to a small enclosure on stilts. Inside were some cages. The squirrel monkey sat on the railing, snatching big blue morpho butterflies from the air and stuffing them into his mouth. Their wings stuck out like a blue mustache.

There were a few injured parrots in the cages, a beautiful

ocelot chained to the railing of the enclosure, and, on the deck, a small, bright blue plastic baby pool filled with water. The old man began to siphon the water out of the pool, revealing an animal's smooth, shiny back. Soon the entire creature lay like a big slug in the empty pool—a baby manatee. Its mother had been illegally killed by local people. The old man smiled sweetly at it as he stuck a big bottle with a nippled end into its whiskered mouth. It closed its eyes and sucked contentedly. When it was through, the old man massaged its body the way its mother would have. Then he refilled the pool with fresh water. The little creature had a look of absolute ecstasy on his face.

That evening as I climbed the tower, I passed the ten scarlet macaws. Further up, a big spider monkey hung by one arm, staring at me—another of the old man's charges.

The next day my boat was waiting in front of the tower. I was getting ready to leave when the old man motioned for me to wait. He came back with an eight-foot boa constrictor and placed it around my neck, like a lei.

SLOTH FAMILY

Amazon River near Manaus, Amazonas, Brazil

The hut sat on stilts at the edge of the brown river, deep in the jungle. It was painted turquoise, with two black window eyes, a door mouth, and a rough wooden dock in front and along one side.

As Wilson, my guide, swung the *panga* (skiff) toward the hut, people appeared in the windows, and the house's eyes seemed to open. A small boy stood on the dock with his little brothers and sister. He was about six years old, with black curly hair and a little potbelly. He looked very shy.

A three-toed sloth hung onto the child's neck, and a baby hung onto *her* neck. The mother sloth looked slowly back and forth between me and the boy, with a face so alien, yet so familiar and sweet. I thought it was odd to see her hanging right side up; in the trees, of course, she would be hanging upside down. I wondered—since she was right side up, did I look upside down to her?

Suddenly the boy handed her and her baby to me. I was

60

touched that he trusted me to hold them. With them came maybe nine hundred or more beetles, mites, ticks, sloth moths, and algae that lived in their fur.

Her fur was grizzled, wiry, and stiff. Whenever her huge, curved claws touched anything, they closed with the force of a vise. What an odd feeling, holding a sloth. I handed her back to the boy. She seemed relieved to be in familiar arms.

"Do you have any money with you?" Wilson asked. I didn't.

He spoke in Portuguese to the people in the windows. They looked disappointed, then withdrew. The eyes of the house closed. Wilson swung the *panga* back into the river.

"I didn't think to bring money," I said. He shrugged.

I looked back at the sloth boy. He waved. I wished I'd had something to give him.

The sloth slowly turned her head toward the sound of the motor. The baby held on tightly.

30

THE GARIMPEIRO

Poconé, Mato Grosso, Brazil

The place looked like a giant anthill with deep trenches gouged out of its hard red soil. Over some of the trenches were crude wooden footbridges.

The *garimpeiro* (gold miner) came out of his hut to greet me. He was big and rough, but seemed oddly distinguished with his long gray hair and trimmed mustache. He wore a wide-brimmed straw hat, striped T-shirt, dirty black shorts, and thongs on his feet. An enormous goiter bulged like another head on the right side of his neck. One of his huge rough hands rested on the shoulder of a slender blond boy about fourteen years old.

The big man took a drag from the cigarette in his other hand, told me to wait, and went behind the hut. He returned, followed by an old orange-and-white dog, with a rough-hewn wooden roller wrapped tightly with stout rope and two battered pails.

He set the roller in a frame on a platform over one of the deepest trenches. Attaching a handle, he lowered the pail into the black pit, thirty-six feet down. "Most of the gold lies below twenty-four feet," he told me.

He cranked the pail back up, full of dirt, and took it to a series of sluices where water was pumped up to wash some of the lighter soil from the heavier parts, which might contain gold. Most of the gold had been taken, he told me. They were now scraping the bottom.

He took the washed soil to an eight-foot-square pond, ankle-deep with red-brown water. The blond boy sat on a stump in the middle of the pond and began to pan.

The big man took a turn at it. He dipped and rotated and lifted the pan, separating the wet soil delicately, with thick fingers. He took a small glass vial out of his shirt pocket and opened it by pulling the top out of it with his teeth. It was full of a liquid like molten silver—mercury. He poured it into the pan, the top still clamped between his teeth. The globule of mercury slid around like a wet slug. When it had separated the gold dust from the soil, he poured the globule back into the palm of his hand, transferred it to the vial, took the gold, and dumped the now mercury-poisoned soil back into the pond.

Inside the hut, he burned off the mercury residue, leaving a tiny cluster of gold worth fourteen dollars. He will take this gold to the government assay office in Poconé, where they will weigh it and give him his money. Mining gold like this is illegal in Brazil. I wonder where they will think he got it?

FRY BREAD

Pyramid Lake, Nevada

The Paiute woman made fry bread wearing surgical gloves. Her grandson sprawled on the couch watching *Willie Wonka and the Chocolate Factory* on the TV. A black cat strutted into the room, tail held high, and began to scratch the couch arm—clearly a work in progress. Then it wandered over to a large wire cage. Inside were two ferrets, curled up together in a tight ball. The cat stuck its paw through the cage bars. One of the ferrets humped forward to sniff it, then crawled up into a cloth sling suspended from the cage sides.

The room was cluttered and the shades drawn. It smelled of death—a sweet, sickening smell.

The Paiute woman made fry bread to sell for gas money. She had to get her husband to Reno for dialysis. He had gangrene in his legs. He was dying.

"These things happen," she said. Still wearing the surgical gloves, she handed me the steaming hot fry bread wrapped tightly in aluminum foil.

AN AMERICAN COWBOY

Jackson, Wyoming

Rex works for one of the local outfitters as a guide and entertainer. He sings cowboy songs and recites cowboy poetry. He calls himself "Rex Roberts: An American Cowboy."

He cuts quite a figure, even among other wranglers. Six feet four, lean with broad shoulders, he walks slightly bent forward. His outfit is classic: collarless shirt, vest, beat-up old short chaps called *chinks,* and a pair of high-heeled boots called *ropers,* which lace all the way up to his knees. He wears a silk bandanna as big as a tablecloth around his neck and a dusty Stetson with a bite out of the brim on his head.

Soft-spoken and gentle, he wears pink-tinted, rimless sunglasses while riding and clear ones when he sings. He has a broken nose and—last but not least, a walrus mustache that hangs over his mouth and, on the sides, droops all the way to his jawbone. Carefully maintained and waxed, it hides, to a degree, his crooked front teeth.

In the off-season, when he's not doing day work for different ranches or packing and guiding for an outfitter, Rex does school programs for kids in cities all over the country. Inner-city kids want to know if he's just a man dressed like a cowboy who's come to entertain them, and if his mustache is real. He tells them about his life, his horse (a red chestnut named Reggie, badly hurt in a trailer accident), and his outfit. He sings some cowboy songs, tells some stories, and for his finale, ropes the vice principal.

On his day off he wanted to show me where he bunked in town, so we headed for the Antler Motel in Jackson. Illuminated only by a bare bulb, the basement room was full of broken hot-water heaters, spare furniture, and a few bikes.

"Here's where I bunk," said Rex, opening the door to an even smaller room. Another bare bulb illuminated a big hot-water heater—it was the boiler room—and two cots. On one of them a cowboy lay flat on his stomach. He still had his boots on—they hung about a foot off the end of the bed, heels up.

"Shoot," said Rex. "He beat me to it! First one here gets the longest bunk."

THE MAN IN THE
COPY SHOP

Brooklyn, New York

"I see you are a writer. I am writing a book about my country, Mozambique—a political book. It's at a university press in Florida, and they wanted lots of money to proofread it. I typed it by hand, no WordPerfect. But they cut my heart in the hospital, and my deadfall [deadline] is past. I didn't have the money."

The phone rang. He picked it up. "Hello, hello . . . who is it that doesn't want to talk to me?" He hung up.

"I have my degree in engineering at the university. My language is Portuguese. When the Russians came, my country decided to be Marxist. Now they're democratic, but they're slaughtering their own educated people."

The phone rang again.

"Somebody else doesn't want to talk to you," I said.

He laughed and picked it up. "Yes . . . yes . . ." He was talking now.

As I left, he said, "Sir, sir, please." I turned. He put his hand over the receiver. "We'll talk again."